ALIEN in my POCKET

Forces of Nature

ALIEN IN MY POCKET

Forces of Nature

by
Nate Ball

illustrated by
Macky Pamintuan

HARPER

An Imprint of HarperCollinsPublishers

Alien in My Pocket: Forces of Nature

Text by Nate Ball, copyright © 2015 by HarperCollins Publishers

Illustrations by Macky Pamintuan, copyright © 2015 by HarperCollins Publishers

All rights reserved. Printed in the United States of America.

www.harpercollinschildrens.com

Library of Congress catalog card number: 2014942415

ISBN 978-0-06-231490-1 (trade bdg.)—ISBN 978-0-06-221633-5 (pbk.)

Typography by Jeff Shake

15 16 17 18 19   OPM   10 9 8 7 6 5 4 3 2 1

❖

First Edition

Contents

01

What a Trip

"The answer is still no," Zack said, stuffing a pair of jeans into the canvas bag that usually held his baseball gear.

"Just think about it," Amp said from atop a pair of rolled-up wool socks that sat on Zack's desk.

"What part of 'no' are you not getting?" Zack asked. "The *n* or the *o* part? It's really a pretty simple word."

Amp stared off into space dreamily. "I've always wanted to go camping," he sighed.

"What?" Zack said, fixing his eyes on his tiny alien roommate. "Yesterday you had never even heard of camping! Now, suddenly, it's your life-long goal? Give me a break, Short Pants."

"We Erdians are fast learners," Amp said with a proud shrug of his little blue shoulders. He folded his arms behind his head and nestled deeper into the sock. "Besides, what an adventure! The chance to battle the elements, the opportunity to encounter wild animals, the daily struggle to find food? Who would pass that up?"

"I already told you, we don't struggle to find food." Zack groaned, pulling a fistful of underwear from an open drawer and tossing it into his bag. "We bring about five hundred pounds of food with us. We're not exactly hunting down beavers with bows and arrows."

Amp sat up and grabbed his antennas with excitement. "And to sleep on the ground in that little cloth house held up by sticks."

"You mean a tent," Zack said flatly.

"Yes!" Amp said, snapping his fingers. "A tent! I want to sleep in a tent."

"Forget it," Zack said, sitting on the corner of his unmade bed and holding his head in his hands. "Quit bugging me about this, okay? You know my family can never know you're here. They'd freak out if they ever saw you. Call the park ranger. Call the cops. Call the government. Not to mention you've still got a little alien invasion to stop.

Remember the whole reason you came to this planet in the first place? You don't want the Erdian Army to arrive only to find their lead scout napping in the woods."

"Come on, a camping trip might be just the thing I need to get the creative juices flowing again."

"It's too risky. If anyone else sees you, they'll take you away and dissect you like a frog."

"But look at the size of me," Amp said, standing up and doing a sort of jumping-jack motion. "I'm so little, they'd never see me. Plus, you know how good I am at staying out of sight."

Zack looked over at Amp and shook his head at his friend's energy.

His family had gone on an annual camping trip for the last three years, and each year had been a disaster. The McGee family just wasn't the outdoorsy type. But every year Zack's dad insisted they go. And every year, a perfectly good three-day weekend was ruined.

Amp fell onto his belly and pressed his face into the fluffy socks. "I promise if you take me with you to the Crooked Forest," his muffled voice begged, "you'll never know I was even there. I'll be like a ninja."

"It's not called the Crooked Forest," Zack said, rolling his eyes. "It's called Twisted Grove State Park."

"Yes! That's it. I want to see the ghost, too," Amp said, rolling onto his back and staring up at the ceiling. "I've never seen a ghost."

"There's no ghost," Zack sighed. "That's just a story people made up."

"You told me the outlaw Nasty Ned hid his stolen gold in that forest over a hundred years

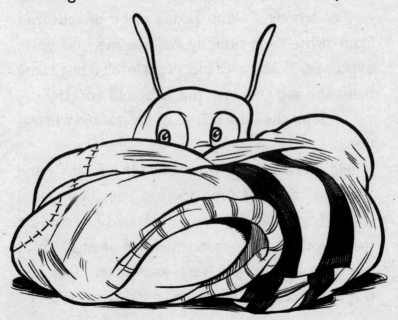

ago, but could never find the spot where he buried it. Now his ghost wanders through the trees at night trying to find it."

"I was just reading you that stuff from the back of the park's map," Zack explained.

Amp sat up. "The anger from Nasty Ned's ghost made all those trees crooked. That's just so exciting."

"But it's not true! It's just something they wrote to make the campgrounds sound mysterious to tourists. It's just a bunch of trees that got bent out of shape. It's no big deal."

"Watch this," Amp said, and he disappeared from sight. "See, nobody will see me," his voice explained. "I'll be invisible. Now let's go hug some trees and see ghosts in the Crooked Forest!"

Zack pinched the bridge of his nose in frustration.

He knew all too well about the Erdian mind trick that enabled Amp to stop your brain from seeing him. The way Amp explained it, he could make your brain forget you were seeing him at the same instant you were seeing him. Zack had trained himself to block the mind trick when he wanted to, but now he just stared at the empty space above the sock.

"Forget it," Zack said, yanking the sock off the desk and stuffing it in his bag. He heard Amp give an invisible cry and then appear just as he crashed onto the desk.

"Ouch!" Amp cried. "That was incredibly rude."

"See, you can't always be invisible," Zack said with a chuckle, zipping up his bag and heading toward the door. "Under the bed are enough Ritz Crackers and SweeTarts to last you a month. I'll be back late on Monday night, okay? Are we good?"

"But I'll be so bored," Amp whined, rubbing the back of his head.

"Just stay in here and out of trouble," Zack said and closed his door.

Alone in the hallway, Zack pressed on the door to make sure it was securely shut, sighed, shook his head, and headed downstairs.

There was one more thing he had to do before leaving.

7

02

The Ol' Switcheroo

"**J**immy has pinkeye," Zack's little brother, Taylor, reported when Zack dropped his bag at the front door. "He can't go camping with us."

"No biggie," Zack said. "More room in the kids' tent."

"But Jimmy always comes with us," Taylor moaned. "He just called. Both his eyes are glued shut with pus."

"Gross! Thanks for sharing, Taylor," Zack said.

Taylor sighed. "This will be our worst camping trip ever."

Zack shrugged. "I'm not so sure. The bar is set pretty low."

"Oh, stop it, you two," Zack's mom said, rolling out a plastic cooler stuffed with ice and food.

"C'mon, Zack, bring this and your bag out to Dad. Olivia is helping him put everything on top of the car."

"Olivia? Why?" Zack asked. Helping Dad tie down the tents and bags was usually his job. He looked out the window and saw Olivia on top of the car, helping Zack's dad thread twine through the handles of various suitcases and tent bags.

Mom brushed Zack's hair from his face with her fingers. "Since Jimmy couldn't go with us, I asked Olivia to come instead. It'll be so fun."

Zack pulled away from his mom. "What?!"

Zack had planned on having Olivia keep an eye on Amp while he was gone. She was the only other person on the planet who knew about Amp, so her going on this trip threw a major wrench into his plans.

Plus, when Zack thought about the close quarters of a tent, camping with Olivia might be a little . . . embarrassing. He flapped his arms, trying to think of something to say. "Mom, I can't sleep in a tent with Olivia. She's a girl. It's just weird!"

"Yeah, Zack likes to fart when he camps," Taylor said. "Nobody should be subjected to his weaponized toots."

"Don't be crude, honey," Mom said to Taylor with a tsk-tsk. "Zack can't help it if he has a sensitive system."

"I don't have a sensitive system," Zack said. "It's just that . . . I don't know. It's just weird, Mom."

What Zack couldn't say was that, while he knew Olivia would make this camping trip a lot

more fun, the thought of leaving Amp unsupervised for a whole three-day weekend made him nervous. Amp was like a disaster magnet.

"Zack also likes to sleep in his underwear," Taylor said. "Now he can't."

"That's not true," Zack said.

Mom continued to try to fix up Zack's hair. "Olivia and I can sleep in the small tent, and you, Taylor, and your father can sleep in the big tent."

"Dad! He snores like a volcano," Zack protested.

"Volcanoes don't snore," Taylor said, shaking his head at his brother's lack of basic science knowledge. "But they do sort of burp. Mostly water vapor and carbon dioxide. But also lots of different sulfur compounds. It's a long list and varies by volcano."

Zack stared at his brother like he was the alien in the house, and then began flapping his arms again. "It's bad enough that Taylor laughs in his sleep, now I get snoring on top of it?"

"I don't laugh in my sleep!" Taylor shouted, apparently insulted at being accused of sleep-laughing.

"She's already coming," Mom said with a firm nod. "Now let's have fun, you two."

What Zack couldn't explain was that Olivia *was* going to feed Mr. Jinxy and walk Smokey while they were gone. Now somebody else would have to come into the house to take care of the cat and the dog, further risking the accidental discovery of Amp.

Zack closed his eyes and shook his head slowly. Camping had always seemed inconvenient, but this year there was so much more at stake.

Zack had a bad feeling about this trip.

He wished he were the one who had come down with pinkeye.

But he was not the lucky type.

03

Carsick

The car ride was long and filled with twists and turns.

Zack kept yawning sleepily to pop his ears as the car climbed into the mountains on a curvy, looping road.

They stopped three times so Taylor could vomit on the side of the road. His carsickness was part of the tradition, and more often than not he wound up vomiting alongside Jimmy. Already the trip felt odd without Taylor's co-vomiter.

After his third puking episode, Taylor fell asleep against Olivia and began laughing. Nothing was creepier than a kid laughing at invisible dreams. It gave Zack the willies.

Zack watched out his window as the trees became bigger and wilder.

Olivia, surprisingly, didn't speak much. Usually she could chatter on about stuff until your ears fell off. But Olivia had never been camping, just fishing and hiking with her grandpa. So, before they left she had grabbed some books about camping from her grandpa's shelf and now she studied them like her life depended on it.

Zack's dad had decided to bring Smokey. Nobody was available on such short notice to

take care of him. He slept on Zack's feet, jerking occasionally while dreaming about squirrels, bacon, or whatever it is that dogs dream about.

Mr. Jinxy wound up being the lucky one. He got to stay home with plenty of food and water, a fresh litter box, and a few balls of yarn to keep him company.

Zack's feet began to fall asleep. He stared out the window. He was worried about Amp. Although Amp was from a far-off, far more advanced civilization, he was lost on Earth. He needed close monitoring and constant attention. And even then, trouble always seemed to follow him. Without Olivia around to watch him, Zack shuddered to think what kind of mischief he could get into.

Zack eventually fell into an uneasy sleep. He dreamed about eating a salami-and-earthworm sandwich at the front of his classroom. He hated that dream.

It was the dream he usually had just before things went terribly wrong.

04

Ranger Davis

"You didn't order a permit for the dog?" a park ranger with a wide-brimmed hat was asking through the open window.

"A what?" Zack's dad asked.

"There's an extra fee to bring a dog to the campgrounds," the ranger explained.

"Oh, well, the girl who was going to watch him while we went camping is now in the backseat," Dad explained.

"Hi, Ranger Davis," Olivia said cheerfully.

"You know him?" Zack croaked.

"His name is on his badge," Olivia said quietly.

Zack pushed Smokey's tail from his face. "We're here already?"

"You and your brother have been sleeping like two big babies," Olivia said.

"And you don't have a reservation number?" Ranger Davis asked.

"I must have forgotten it," Dad said, looking around lamely.

"This happens every year," Zack mumbled to Olivia.

"One moment," Ranger Davis said crisply. He entered his little ranger hut.

"Last name is McGee!" Zack's mom called after him. "Isn't this fun, kids?" she asked.

They all sat quietly, the car idling, Smokey panting, his terrible breath nearly melting Zack's eyeballs.

Zack noticed that Taylor was fingering a small pair of binoculars. His binoculars! "Those aren't my binoculars, are they?" he asked with a hollow voice.

"Relax, they're for bird-watching," Taylor said. "Mom said I could borrow them."

"You went in my room?" Zack shouted, leaning across Olivia and grabbing Taylor by the sleeve.

"Take it easy, Zack," Mom said from the front seat. "I told him he could borrow them, sweetie."

"But they're mine!" Zack said. "You should

have asked me! Did you close my bedroom door?"

"Why?" Taylor said, trying to pull away. "What's your problem?"

"What's your bedroom door got to do with anything?" Dad asked, peering back at him in the rearview mirror.

"Uh-oh," Olivia whispered.

"Did you close my door?" Zack asked Taylor again. "Yes or no?"

Zack's mom snapped her fingers at him. "Zack, you're squishing Olivia!"

"Is there a problem here?" Ranger Davis asked, reappearing at the window.

"Tell me now, did you leave my door open or not?" Zack hissed at Taylor through gritted teeth. "It's a matter of life and death!"

"It is?" Taylor said, his face wrinkled up in disgust. "Why?"

"Stop the monkey business back there," Dad barked.

"Did . . . you . . . leave . . . my . . . door . . . open?" Zack grunted.

"I guess," Taylor said. "I don't know. I can't remember."

The ranger tapped his clipboard on the open window. "Folks, is everything okay?"

"I CAN'T BELIEVE THIS!!" Zack shouted. "I LEAVE MY DOOR SHUT!"

"What's the big deal, honey?" Zack's mom said.

"Mr. Jinxy could get him," Zack told Olivia.

"Get who?" Mom asked.

"Folks, please," Ranger Davis said.

"Or he could get out," Olivia whispered.

"I was afraid of this," Zack said, grabbing a fistful of his own hair. "If there's trouble to be found, he'll find it."

"Who could get out?" Mom asked. "Who could find trouble? Mr. Jinxy?"

"Would everybody just pipe down!" Dad roared.

"Maybe everybody should get out of the car and have a time-out," Ranger Davis said.

"Sorry, officer," Dad said, "the kids get cranky after a long drive."

"We run a nice, friendly campground here and—" Ranger Davis's face froze. He scrunched up his face. His lip quivered and his left eye closed.

"Yikes. Did you folks bring eggs with you? I smell rotten eggs, real bad."

Zack and Olivia exchanged a glance of horror.

"Oh no," Zack said.

Ranger Davis pulled off his hat and waved it in front of his watery eyes. "Whew! Here, take it," he gasped, handing Dad a sheet of paper. "Campsite thirteen. Take the second left. It's the very last one on that road, just past the narrow bridge." He stumbled back from the car.

"Thank you," Dad said, taking the paper and putting the car into drive. He pulled the car forward. "What was that all about? Does anybody else smell eggs?"

"Probably Zack tooting already," Taylor said, glancing sideways at his brother.

"We don't smell anything," Olivia said, staring at Zack with a look of alarm.

The alleged egg smell could only mean one thing: they had a stowaway. Amp was somewhere in this car! One of Amp's favorite Erdian mind tricks involved convincing people they could smell or taste things—usually gross things.

Zack pressed his fists into his eyes. This is exactly what he was afraid of. He shook his head in disbelief.

Olivia patted Zack's shoulder as the car moved slowly over the gravel road. "Did you hear that, Zack? We're at campsite number thirteen. Some people would consider that unlucky." She poked him in the ribs, but she couldn't get him to smile or squirm.

"I'm gonna strangle that pipsqueak for disobeying a direct order," Zack growled quietly.

The Site

"When Ranger Davis said it was the last camp-site on this road, he wasn't kidding," Olivia said.

"Lucky number thirteen," Zack said, staring at the small sign with a faded and chipped *13* painted on it.

They were a good hundred yards past the second-to-last campsite. The trees soared around them, forming a dark canopy that hung gloomily over them. The sound of a nearby creek provided the only noise in the hushed surroundings.

"I think I see a bird!" Taylor shrieked and ran into the trees.

"Honey, don't run while looking through the binoculars," Mom called out after him.

"My binoculars won't make it through the weekend," Zack said to Olivia.

Dad was yanking the tents off the top of the car. Smokey was visiting each tree surrounding campsite thirteen and peeing on it.

Zack shook his head. They hadn't seen Amp yet, but he was here somewhere. Zack looked over at Olivia. "He'll probably get eaten by a badger."

"There aren't badgers around here, Ranger Zack, but there are bears." Olivia held up the sheet Ranger Davis had handed to Zack's dad. It was a warning about bears invading your camp-site and directions on how to properly store your food to avoid it. There was also a set of campsite rules and a small map of the campsites. It had the number 13 scrawled on the top in thick, black ink.

"I have a bad feeling about this trip," Zack said, staring at the cartoon of a bear with its snout stuck in a cookie jar. Drops began hitting the paper as he looked at it. A slow, steady, light rain began falling around them. Zack looked up and drops fell onto his face. "See, I told you. When it rains it pours."

"Your dad is setting up the tents in the wrong place."

"What? What do you mean?"

"Look, he's picked the flattest area, but that's the low point. It will fill up with rainwater and turn to mud during the night. He's got to move uphill if it's going to be raining."

Zack stared at his dad struggling to pull the tents out of their bags. "You better go tell him. He won't listen to me if I say something. Last year both tents collapsed on the first night."

"It's raining!" Taylor shrieked from the trees, as if he had never seen rain before.

"Don't shout, honey," Mom called out to him from the back of the car. "You'll scare the birds."

Zack groaned. He knew that Amp was hiding. He knew Zack would be mad, so he was making himself scarce. "Amp thinks there's a ghost in these woods."

"You didn't read the back of the park's brochure to him, did you?"

"I wasn't thinking."

"I'll say. You know how excited he gets about that stuff. All those old horror movies you guys watch are coming back to haunt you. Amp told me he wants to see a vampire, a mummy, and a zombie before he goes back to his planet."

Zack shook his head. "He knows there are no zombies and ghosts. He just hates to be left out, so he ignored a direct order. So frustrating."

Olivia grinned. "You're starting to sound like your parents."

"Oh my gosh!" Zack's mom shrieked from behind the car. She took several quick steps back. "It smells like dog poop back here all of sudden! Zack? Come here and smell this!"

Zack looked at Olivia. "Looks like my mom found him, or almost found him. That trick is going to get old real quick if he keeps using it."

"I'll go talk to your dad. You help your mom and get your hands on that Erdian."

Just then a strange, far-off animal noise filled the air. It wasn't exactly a howl, but it wasn't a grunt or a growl or a bark either. It wasn't made by a person, that was clear. Everyone stopped and looked in the direction it had come from. Smokey sniffed the air.

"What was that?!" Taylor squealed, dropping

Zack's binoculars into the dirt and running to his dad's side.

"Sounded like a werewolf to me," Olivia said.

Zack looked at Olivia in disbelief. "Now Amp will want to see a werewolf!"

Olivia shrugged. "Hey, maybe he will." She walked off to help Dad.

Zack kept his eyes on the area of the forest where the sound had come from. Now he had to add the chance of being eaten by a werewolf to his list of concerns.

06

First-Night Blues

"**Z**ack?"

Zack woke with a start. He blinked and saw nothing. It was as black as space inside the tent. Without stars.

But unlike space, it was not silent.

His dad's tent-shaking snore filled the air approximately every six seconds. His brother's giggles, chuckles, and random fits of laughter were more irregular. They came out of nowhere, lasted longer, and were far more disturbing than Mr. Thundersnore.

Adding to the concert of snoring and random sleep-laughing was the constant pitter-patter-pitter-patter of rain on the tent.

It was like trying to sleep inside a drum.

"Zack?"

This time there was no mistaking it. Amp was calling his name.

But that didn't mean that Amp was in the tent.

Amp could speak directly into Zack's brain, sort of like a mind-to-mind cell phone call. Zack hated when Amp communicated this way. It gave him the willies, sort of like putting on wet socks . . . if your brain had feet. Zack could never describe the feeling accurately in words.

Now he sat up and looked around like a blind man. He could talk back to Amp without speaking out loud. He just had to think the words very hard. "Where have you been hiding, Amp?" he thought. "I told you to stay home! You never listen!"

Taylor laughed in the darkness. His dad snored. Zack shook his head in frustration.

"What are you doing?" Amp said casually inside his head.

"What do you think I'm doing? It's the middle of the night! I'm trying to sleep. What are you doing here? You were supposed to stay home!"

"Which tent are you in?" Amp's voice echoed in Zack's head.

33

"I'm in the one making all the weird noises! Why?"

"Can I come in?"

Zack shook his head in the darkness. "We're not really entertaining guests at the moment. We're wedged in here like cats in a bag."

"But I'm soaked and hungry and cold and covered in mud."

"It serves you right. I told you camping was no place for an alien the size of a pear."

Amp was quiet for a full thirty seconds before he responded. "Do you think of me as pear-shaped? That's not exactly a compliment."

Zack grabbed his head. All this talking in his brain was giving him a headache. "It's just the first thing that came into my mind."

"A mango would at least be less insulting. Or a short banana," Amp said inside Zack's head. "When I stand up tall I could be almost banana-shaped, don't you think?"

Zack groaned. "Get outta my skull! It's closed for the night. I'm not discussing fruit anymore. But, frankly, you're pretty much a grapefruit."

"Okay, now that was just hurtful."

Zack made fists and stared up into the blackness. He clenched his teeth. Taylor snickered suddenly. His dad snored right on schedule. Zack was waiting. He knew Amp wouldn't stop. He wondered for a moment if a fourth grader could get gray hair. He just might be the first.

"Now what are you doing?" Amp asked.

Zack sat up and punched his sleeping back with both fists. "This is a disaster!" he mind-bombed Amp. "These two could wake up at any second."

"Doesn't sound like it," Amp commented quietly inside Zack's head.

"Oh, so now you're a sleep expert? You don't even need to sleep."

"This isn't what I pictured camping would be like," Amp said.

Zack simmered in the darkness. This situation was impossible. The rain seemed to have slowed down to a trickle. His sleeping bag was between his dad's and brother's, so he had to lean far over his brother's body to reach the zipper on the tent's door. He pulled it up quietly as a rush of cool, moist air entered the tent.

"Finally," Amp said out loud.

"Shhhh!" Zack said. He could barely see Amp's tiny, muddy figure enter the tent and move to the side. Zack pulled the tent's zipper back down as quietly as he could, shutting off the flow of cool air.

"Whew! It's much warmer in here," Amp whispered cheerfully.

"Glad you like it," Zack said quietly.

"Say, anything to eat? Ritz Crackers? Swee-Tarts?"

"No," Zack said, falling back onto his small camping pillow. "Now stay out of sight, or things will really get really uncomfortable for you."

Amp whispered in the dark.

"Note to Erdian Council . . ."

"Now? Are you kidding me?"

Amp often recorded his observations about Earth into a tiny device on his wrist. He had explained to Zack it was one of his duties as an Erdian scout. It drove Zack crazy every single time.

Amp made no effort to talk quietly.

"When camping, humans rest their brains while inside a thin, flimsy cloth structure."

"It's called a tent," Zack hissed.
Amp continued.

**"Still cannot determine why
they go camping as the humans
seem uncomfortable and miserable
without the comforts of their more
sturdy, wooden structures."**

"Those are called houses," Zack moaned.

**"More observations of this
strange human ritual to come later.
This is Scout Amp signing off."**

Zack shook his head in the dark and finally drifted off into a deep and uneasy sleep filled with troubling dreams about fruit salad and snakes.

07

Washed Out

"**P**ssst!"

Zack's eyes popped open. The tent was filled with a dim light that told Zack it was early in the morning. Everything felt damp. The cold air was moist and misty. He remembered Amp was in the tent and he hoped that nobody had rolled over on him and crushed him into a flat, blue pancake.

"Pssst!"

He sat up. That wasn't Amp. That was Olivia. He had forgotten she was even on this trip.

"Zack?" he heard Olivia ask from outside the tent.

Taylor turned over and sat up, still looking mid-dream. "What happened?" he croaked. His hair shot up into the air, making him look like a rooster that had missed the sunrise.

"Don't wake Dad," Zack whispered.

"What is it, Olivia?" Dad said, stirring in the sleeping bag next to Zack. "Everything okay out there?"

"Which one of you made this fire?"

The three tentmates exchanged puzzled glances. They all had clearly just woken up, so it wasn't them.

"I thought it was a forest fire," Zack's mom said from somewhere outside.

Taylor unzipped the tent, letting in a blast of chilly air. He stepped outside in his bare feet. "It wasn't us!" he exclaimed. "WOW!"

Zack looked at his dad and the two crawled to the tent's opening and poked their heads out.

Between the tents a giant campfire roared. They stared in stunned silence, blinking from the heat.

It looked like a campfire, but it was way larger than it needed to be. Zack could feel the heat on his face from twelve feet away.

"If we didn't build it," Zack's dad said quietly, "and you didn't build it . . . who built it?"

Zack looked over at Olivia and they shared a troubled look.

"It must have been built by the ghost," Taylor squealed with excitement. "Nasty Ned must have built it."

"Don't be ridiculous," Zack said. "It was probably Ranger Davis."

"I don't think rangers make fires for you," Olivia said. "It's not like a hotel. And I don't think a ranger would make a fire this big and danger-ous."

"Quick, Mom, get the marshmallows!" Tay-lor shrieked, his feet squishing in the mud as he stepped closer to the fire and held up his hands. "This is the best day ever!"

"Be quiet, Taylor, you'll wake up the owls," Zack said.

"Not too close, honey," Mom said, stepping closer to Taylor nervously.

"Let's go get the ranger," Dad suggested, clearly shaken by the sudden, strange campfire. "It's not safe here."

Of course, Zack and Olivia couldn't say any-thing for fear of giving away the fact that their alien friend was surely behind this fire. In a matter of minutes, Olivia and the McGee family were in the car, their hiking boots, coats, and wool caps thrown on in a hurry.

Soon the car was slipping and sliding down the muddy road. Zack watched as the flames died down, so he didn't see that the narrow bridge that ran over the small creek near the campsite was gone.

But Olivia did—and just in time.

"NO BRIDGE!" she screamed. "STOP!"

Dad stomped on the brake pedal. The tires skidded over the mud like a sled, and the car's rear end swung out to one side, then back in the other direction. Zack's mom screeched in fear.

The car stopped with just feet to spare.

They all sat in eerie silence for a few seconds, then quickly exited the car to check on the bridge's destruction. They walked to the edge of the now-roaring stream in silence, staring down at the bubbling water. The muddy liquid was violently pushing over the splintered posts that once held up the little wooden bridge.

"We're stuck here?" Taylor shouted. "Awesome!"

"Incredible," Dad said, staring down at the remains of the bridge and the foaming, churning water.

"Maybe the ghost wrecked the bridge after he built us a fire," Taylor said.

"This is all getting too dangerous," Mom said,

putting her hand on Taylor's shoulder to keep him from wandering too close to the water's edge.

Dad pulled out his cell phone and stared at it. "No service out here," he said.

"And I thought last year's trip was a disaster," Zack said.

"Uh, guys, we have a visitor," Olivia announced in an odd, pinched voice.

Zack noticed that Olivia was looking back at the car.

Everyone slowly turned around and watched as a massive brown bear squeezed itself into the front seat of the car.

08

New Friends

Despite the bear that was growling at them from his family car, Zack still heard the splash loud and clear.

It sounded like a giant boulder had been thrown into the water.

But it was no boulder.

Zack's mom had fallen into the water, probably when she had turned to run away from the bear.

Mom had a tendency to panic.

Mrs. McGee also wasn't much of a swimmer. She bobbed and gasped before getting hold of a log that was floating down the river along with her. She held on to it as she was swept along in water that could be no deeper than four or five feet.

Zack's dad now ran along the stream shouting at her as she was carried downstream. "Just stand up! Just stand up!"

He had forgotten about the bear.

And his car.

And Zack, Taylor, and Olivia.

Apparently, Zack's dad wasn't great in emergencies either.

Really the McGees simply were not the outdoorsy type.

Zack was about to mention this to Olivia, but before he could utter a word, another even larger bear stepped out from behind the passenger side.

This bear looked surprised when it saw the three bug-eyed kids standing at the edge of the creek.

It stopped and sniffed the air with interest. Its head swung back and forth. Then it pushed off its massive front paws, stood up, and made a growly, groaning noise.

Zack was pretty sure this was the sound they had heard coming from the forest last night.

No bear ever looked this big in the zoo, but that was probably because there was always a nice, sturdy wall between you and those finger-size front fangs.

"Should we run?" he whispered to Olivia without taking his eyes off the bear.

"Don't run," Olivia said sharply. "Are you crazy? It'll make you look like a snack in sneakers."

"Should we jump into the creek?"

"That will make you look like a delicious trout."

"Okay, how about if we just lie down and play dead?" Zack said, barely moving his lips.

"Well, you may end up not playing dead, and actually become dead."

"Okay, Ranger Olivia, what do you think we should do?"

Without answering, Olivia started to wave her arms and whistle as loud as she could. Zack watched her out of the corner of his eye.

"What the—?"

"Don't you ever read, Zack?" she shouted at the bear, her arms continuing to flap. "The ranger's sheet said to look big, make noise, and retreat only when it's safe."

Zack started to wave his arms and jump up

and down. "HEY, YOU BIG, FAT, UGLY BEAR! YOU STINK LIKE BEAR FARTS!"

"Don't insult the animal!" Olivia snapped.

"I don't think it speaks English," Zack replied, his arms waving crazily above his head.

Taylor hadn't moved an inch since the appearance of the bear. "This is the best trip ever," Zack heard him mumble.

The bear seemed to lose interest in the kids. It dropped down heavily onto its front paws, turned around, and entered the front passenger door. The car rocked from the weight of the second bear.

Zack could hear the *bing-bong* chiming of the alarm inside the car that signaled to the driver that the door was open and the key still in the ignition. The car engine was still on.

"Okay, now run!" Olivia said and shot down the side of the creek in the opposite direction from where Zack's parents had gone.

"What if they steal our car?" Zack asked, instantly realizing it was a dumb question.

Zack was stunned to see Taylor already a good seventy-five yards away from them, running

along the stream in the same direction Zack's dad had run. "WAIT!" Zack shouted. But Taylor was gone.

The bears were now ripping off the top of a blue plastic cooler they had found in the car. The lid of the cooler and a few dozen ice cubes tumbled out of the driver's-side door and fell into the mud. Zack knew it was the one filled with foil-wrapped steaks. Tomorrow night's dinner was being served early. And uncooked.

That's when Zack saw another bear emerge from some trees and gallop toward the car.

He ran after Olivia and didn't look back again.

He didn't know exactly how, but he knew for certain that somehow Amp was responsible for this mess.

Meltdown

"This is Amp's fault," Zack gasped, his hands on his knees, trying his best to catch his breath.

"How do you figure?" Olivia said, leaning her back on a tree.

They were standing in a small clearing carpeted with pine needles. The soaring trees around them dimmed what little light was able to get through the dark rain clouds above. They had run along the creek for as long as they could and now they stood huffing and puffing after putting a good mile or two between them and the bears.

"Oh, please. Amp totally started that fire," Zack said.

"We don't know that for sure," she answered.

"C'mon, Olivia, this mess has his tiny fingerprints all over it."

Olivia kicked a pinecone with her muddy sneaker. "Okay, maybe it was, but he was only trying to be helpful."

"Our tents are probably melted hunks of plastic right now. Thanks a lot, Amp."

"You're always so hard on him," Olivia sighed. "He means well." Olivia snapped her fingers. "Hey, you guys talk with your minds all the time. So just tell him to get his tushy over here."

"He won't know what the word *tushy* even means," Zack groaned, pressing his forehead onto the rough bark of a tree.

"C'mon, squirt out one of your mental phone calls. We're in a jam here. We need some Erdian backup."

Zack rolled his eyes. "You know you can talk to him that way, too, but you just don't like to."

"It makes my skin crawl. You're good at it. You two do it all the time."

"He's probably out of range. I've got to be within fifty yards or so. There are no long-distance calls. His brain is probably the size of a peanut. His peanut brain has a very limited range."

Olivia stared at her friend for a moment.

"You've got some serious anger issues, you know."

"What is the point of camping anyway?" Zack roared, holding up his arms. "Weren't we perfectly happy with carpet under our feet, our comfortable beds, and cable television? Now I've got a blister on my heel that's killing me, our campsite has been burned to the ground, my mom's probably been washed out to the ocean, and a pack of bears has taken the family car. Whoop-de-do! I can't wait for next year's camping trip!"

Olivia looked away for a moment. "A group of bears is called a sleuth."

"What?"

"You said 'a pack of bears.' Technically, or scientifically, it's called a sleuth of bears."

"Are you trying to make me cry?"

"Hey, Zack, look up."

Zack followed Olivia's eyes and looked straight up at the soaring trees around them. He noticed that they were all twisted, like corkscrews. Unlike most trees, which grew up straight toward the sun, these trees were bent at odd angles, their bark wrapping around the trunks as if the trees themselves were confused about which way was up.

"Twisted Grove State Park," Zack whispered, the trees giving him an uneasy feeling.

"Kinda creepy," Olivia said quietly.

They continued to stare up at the strange trees in silence. Besides a few chirping birds and the hiss of the rushing water in the nearby creek, it would have been perfectly quiet, which made the twisted trees all the more troubling for some reason.

"Too bad Amp's not here," Olivia said.

"Yeah," Zack agreed quietly. "He'd love this."

Olivia sipped water from a plastic bottle she pulled from her coat. "Maybe we'll meet the ghost of Nasty Ned out here."

Zack made a disapproving noise. "C'mon, let's circle around through the woods and work our way back to the campsite. Maybe my parents and Taylor are back there by now."

"Lead the way, Nasty Ned," Olivia said with a salute, then followed Zack as he marched across the small clearing and into the dark woods.

It would be well over an hour before Zack would realize that he had been leading the way in the wrong direction.

10

Lost in the Woods

"I think I know how those trees back there became crooked," Olivia said as she followed Zack through the dim woods.

"Let me guess," Zack said, "you think it was anger from Nasty Ned's ghost that made those trees go all twisty."

"No, that's ridiculous," Olivia said. "But I have a hypothesis."

"What's a hypothesis?"

"Seriously?"

Zack looked back over his shoulder and saw the sour face Olivia was making. "Yeah. What's a hypothesis? Sorry, is that something everyone knows?"

"You know what a hypothesis is," Olivia said, stepping over a log. "It's like an idea for how you think something works."

Zack shook his head. "Nope. Strike two. I don't know what a hypothesis is."

"Are you even listening? Remember when we did our experiments for the science fair?"

"Oh, please don't remind me. I've been trying to forget that for weeks."

Zack stopped and looked up at the small patch of dark clouds he could see between the trees.

He thought they would have been back to their campsite by now.

He looked back in the direction they had come, took a deep breath, then began to climb a steep hill in front of them. The hill was covered with fallen trees and tall plants covered with purple flowers. He had the feeling they had already climbed this hill about forty minutes earlier.

Olivia picked some of the flowers and made a tiny bouquet as she followed Zack. "So anyway," she said, "remember how you first have to come up with a hypothesis, which is sort of like a guess about how something works? Then you do an experiment to prove or disprove your hypothesis. It's called the scientific method."

"Yeah, that kinda rings a bell," Zack said with a shrug.

"Oh my gosh, how could you forget that? You live with a science geek from another planet!"

"Maybe that's why I don't like to think about this stuff. I might be allergic to science. It makes me itchy."

"That's ridiculous."

"Sorry, I was born this way. Don't judge."

"Anyway, my hypothesis goes like this. Those trees once grew straight up to the sky, like every other tree. But a long time ago, there was an earthquake, a landslide, or the soil that they were growing on just shifted downhill, toward the river."

"You mean the creek."

"Whatever. Anyway, the trees moved from their original position. Their orientation in relation to the sun and the sky changed. The trees don't know any better, so they start growing back toward the sky."

"Trees can't move that fast."

"These changes would be very slow. They would take decades."

"That's ten years, right? A decade?"

"Oh my gosh. Yes! Those trees are probably over two hundred years old, so the ground back there has probably shifted several times, which is why they didn't grow straight up. That's my hypothesis on how they got twisted like that."

"Interesting hypothesis," Zack said, grunting

as he finally reached the top of the hill. "But my hypothesis is that it was the anger that comes from Nasty Ned's ghost. Though either way, I don't have two hundred years to wait around for experimental results."

They stood in silence at the top of the hill they had just climbed, breathing heavily. They looked around in silence. They both spun slowly in circles.

"I'd swear we've been here before," Olivia said.

"I thought we'd be back at our campsite by now," Zack said.

"I have a new hypothesis," Olivia said, plucking petals from the bouquet.

"Me, too. We're totally lost."

"Yup, that was my hypothesis. We've been going in circles, haven't we?"

"I don't think we even need to prove it with an experiment."

Just then a strange animal noise from an uncomfortably nearby distance filled the air. It wasn't exactly a howl, but it wasn't a grunt or a growl or a bark either.

Olivia took a quick step closer to Zack. "What was that?"

It was the same sound they had heard coming from the woods when they had arrived at their campsite. Zack and Olivia turned in the direction the noise had come from.

"It's Nasty Ned," Zack whispered.

"It's that werewolf," Olivia said quietly. "It's been nice knowing you, McGee."

They were silent for a full minute and didn't hear another noise.

"We're lost in the woods and surrounded by hungry werewolves," Zack finally whispered. "And my dad can't figure out why I don't like camping."

Olivia dropped the tiny bouquet of flowers and grabbed Zack firmly by the shoulders. "I know you said you can't make long-distance calls with Amp using your brain, but you need to try. Try really hard. We need Amp's help and we need it now."

"The fact that we're relying on my brain worries me more than that hungry monster sound we just heard," Zack said.

"Shut up and make the call," Olivia said, "before you become a Zackburger."

11

Loud Silence

"**W**hat's wrong?"

Zack opened his eyes. "What?"

"Do you have to go to the bathroom or something?"

"No! Why?"

Olivia shrugged. "I don't know. It looked like you were having some kind of an episode."

"An episode?"

"Yeah. Your face was all scrunched up, and you're kinda . . . squatting a little bit."

Zack bugged out his eyes. "Have you ever tried to shout silently? Using only your mind? It's not easy."

"Listen, if you need to go the bathroom, I can—"

"All this mental yelling is melting my brain."

He shook his head. "I'm not hearing anything from Amp."

Olivia looked around at the surrounding woods. "What if we're lost overnight?"

"I have two flashlights," Zack said.

"Oh, thank goodness."

"But not with me. One is in the tent, which is probably burned to a crisp by now. And the other one was in the car, which was taken for a joyride by a gang of hungry bears."

"A *sleuth* of hungry bears."

"Whatever."

"Well, thanks for telling me about the flashlights you don't have. Really helpful," Olivia said, punching Zack too hard in the arm.

Zack rubbed his arm and looked back down the hill they had climbed earlier. "Maybe we should just—" Zack stopped and held up both hands. "Wait. I just heard something."

"You did?" Olivia said, her eyes darting around. "Bears?"

"No, in my head. I just heard—"

Olivia clapped excitedly. "Is it Amp? I don't hear anything. What did he say? Did he sound—"

Zack shushed Olivia again. Zack thought, "AMP! IS THAT YOU? WHERE ARE YOU, YOU ERDIAN PIPSQUEAK?"

"Zack?" a faint voice said in his head.

"I can hear him," Zack said to Olivia.

"Make some noise," Amp echoed in Zack's head. "I'll find you."

"He wants us to make noise!" Zack shouted in Olivia's face. He started howling, clapping, whistling, and jumping around in circles. Olivia joined him. The two made a racket that seemed to hush the forest around them.

"I see you!" Amp said in both their heads.

"I heard him! He sees us!" Olivia roared. "We're saved!"

The two stopped making noise and spun in circles, looking for the arrival of their rescue party.

But what emerged from the bushes behind them didn't look like a rescue party.

It was one of the strangest sights Zack had ever seen, and he had seen his share of weird things for a fourth grader.

Zack's dog Smokey suddenly appeared from behind a tree, tail wagging. Zack crouched to greet him and that's when he saw Amp sitting on Smokey's neck, holding firmly to the dog's flea collar.

Zack stared at his tiny alien roommate. "You're riding my dog?"

"An alien riding dogback," Olivia said. "And I thought I'd seen everything."

"I can steer this animal quite easily with my mind," Amp said with delight. "This animal is actually quite reasonable, especially when compared to that beastly cat of yours."

Olivia laughed. "Gosh, Amp, you hacked into

the brain of Zack's dog. Kind of rude, no?"

Zack shook his head. "I don't even care at this point," Zack said, standing and brushing off his pants. "C'mon, Amp, we need to get back to our campsite and find Mom, Dad, and Taylor. Lead the way."

Amp looked up at Zack, then at Olivia, then back to Zack. "Me? You don't know which way to go?"

"No!" Olivia roared. "Now take us back to camp! I'm starving."

"Wait, you're lost?" Amp said, confused. "So am I! I've been riding this animal in circles through the forest since everyone ran off this morning. I thought you two could take me back to—"

"Oh, great," Zack moaned, his chin dropping to his chest. "Our rescue party is more lost than we are."

Olivia sighed and squeezed her face between her hands. "Now what are we supposed to do?"

"Hey, it's your planet," Amp said with a tiny shrug. "I have no idea. I thought you two were rescuing *me*!"

"I *really* hate camping," Zack said.

12

Directionless

"**T**hat fire you built freaked us out," Zack said.

"Oh dear," Amp said. "I wasn't sure how big to make it."

"There's a difference between a campfire and a forest fire," Olivia said.

"I said I was sorry!" Amp cried, throwing up his hands in surrender. "I headed out on your dog this morning after I made the fire to see if I could communicate with the bears."

"Bears? You could have gotten Smokey eaten!" Zack cried, scratching Smokey behind the ears. He plucked up Amp and held him in the palm of his hand. Smokey seemed to shake off Amp's mind control then and started sniffing around.

Zack and Olivia told Amp all about their shock at the big fire, the washed-out bridge, Zack's mom's plunge into the creek, the bears entering the car through the open car doors, and their poorly planned escape.

Zack slapped at a mosquito that had landed on his cheek. "See, this is why I didn't want you to come, Amp," Zack said. "You're way out of your element."

"Oh, this is pretty tame compared to other planets I've been on," Amp said casually, looking around at the forest. "I was on a planet once where the trees spit big gobs of sap on you as you walked by them."

"That is so gross," Olivia said, placing a hand on her stomach.

"And that sap was toxic; it had acid in it! Melted right through my helmet."

Zack often forgot that Amp had been to places he couldn't even imagine, which made it all the harder to believe he could make such a mess of things on a simple camping trip.

"That's fascinating, Amp," Zack sighed. "But let's focus on the fact that we need to get back, and we're totally lost."

"When it gets dark, we'll be totally blind out

here," Olivia said.

"Yes," Amp said, looking from Zack's face to Olivia's. "If only I had my spaceship."

"If only I had a helicopter!" Zack said. "Or a trail of bread crumbs that led me back to our campsite."

"If only I had a turkey sandwich," Olivia said dreamily.

Zack's stomach growled.

Amp stroked his chin and made his thinking face. "If only we had a map."

They all nodded in silence.

"Wait a second!" Olivia shouted. She reached into her back pocket and pulled out a folded-up piece of paper. She unfolded it and held it up for Amp and Zack to see. "This has a map on it!"

"It's the paper Ranger Davis gave us!" Zack cried. "Why'd it take you so long to remember it?"

"I forgot I had it," Olivia said simply, "until Amp said that about a map."

Zack put Amp down so he could examine the map closely. "This is a very simple, crude map. All the park rules and this drawing of a bear eating from a cookie jar take up most of the space. Not sure it will help us."

The three of them studied that small map. Zack saw the number 13 that Ranger Davis had written on it. He found the matching campsite 13 on the little map. "We were way down here, at this campsite, number thirteen. We started back up the road this way, but this little line must be the creek, and the bridge was gone."

"So we ran this way, away from the bears," Olivia said, tracing her finger along the line of the creek. "And ended up somewhere in this area, where it says Crooked Tree Grove."

"Oh, you saw the trees!" Amp exclaimed, shaking his head in disappointment. "I wanted to see those."

"You would have really liked it," Olivia said, giving him a pained grin.

Zack continued. "Then we walked in this direction, which I thought would bring us the back way to campsite number thirteen, but I must have misjudged it. Or just didn't go in a straight line. We could be anywhere." He looked at Olivia. "Sorry, Olivia."

Olivia shrugged. "Hey, I didn't notice either, so . . ."

"Well, this is good news," Amp said.

"It is?" Zack and Olivia said at the same time.

"Jinx," Olivia said. She quickly punched Zack on the arm, in the exact same spot she had punched him earlier.

The impact caused Zack to jerk back and Amp nearly fell off Zack's upturned palm. He now clung to Zack's pinky finger, his body swinging underneath. "Could you two be a bit more careful?"

It was one of Olivia's unwritten rules of life: if two people said the same thing at the same time, one of you got to punch the other one for free, and the punched party was not allowed to retaliate.

"Sorry," Olivia said, and she grabbed Amp and put him back on Zack's palm.

Zack rotated his arm stiffly and shook his head at Olivia. "Why is all that good news, Amp?" Zack said. "We have a map, yes, but we don't know where we are on that map."

"Yeah," Olivia said. "Too bad it doesn't have one of those red dots that says 'You are here.'"

"It's simple," Amp said, studying the map with great interest. "Zack, because of your poor sense of direction, you obviously led Olivia out into this empty space on the map. Now look at this small compass rose here."

"What's a compass rose?" Zack asked.

Amp pointed to a triangle with an N on top of it. "It's a small graphic, icon, or symbol that tells you which way is north," Amp explained. "Most maps have them."

"Cool," Zack said, nodding his head, impressed. "So if we just go north, we'll run right into campsite thirteen."

"Exactly," Amp said, lifting his chin in the air.

"Knuckle bump," Zack said, holding up a fist. "Who's my alien?"

Amp made a small fist, and bumped his tiny knuckles off Zack's. They both opened their hands afterward and made the sound of something blowing up.

"Uh, fellas," Olivia said, "how are we supposed to know which way is north?"

Zack stared at Amp. Amp stared at Zack. Silence filled the air.

Amp's look of triumph faded away and his puffed-up chest seemed to deflate. "Oh, I didn't think of that. Olivia is right. Without a compass, we're no better off."

Just then, the same far-off animal noise filled the air.

They all looked in the direction the sound had come from.

"Well," Zack sighed, "we better think of

something fast before we get eaten."

"They'll probably start with you, Amp," Olivia said, nudging Amp with her index finger. "You're like an appetizer."

Don't Drink That!

"Okay, on three you guys point in the direction you think is north," Zack said. "One, two, three!"

Each of them pointed in a completely different direction.

"Oh my," Amp said.

Zack and Olivia were sitting on the ground, legs crossed, facing each other. Olivia had put the sheet of paper with the map on the ground between them. Amp now paced around on top of it. Zack petted a sleeping and exhausted Smokey. Olivia sipped from her water bottle.

"I know the sun sets in the west," Olivia said, "but with all these trees and those heavy clouds, who knows which way that is."

"I once heard that moss will grow on only

one side of a tree," Zack said, "but I forgot which side, and none of these trees have moss on them."

"I'm not used to not having any of my tools," Amp said, nervously wringing his tiny hands. "I shouldn't have come. You were right, Zack. I've made a mess of everything."

"Don't worry, I'm used to it," Zack said, slapping a mosquito into the back of his neck.

"Think! Think! Think!" Amp said, pounding a little fist on his forehead.

"Can I have a sip?" Zack asked Olivia. "My tongue feels like a dead weasel."

"Don't let it touch your lips," Olivia said, reluctantly handing over the bottle. "Just sort of waterfall it."

"Afraid of my cooties?" Zack asked.

"No, your gross diseases," Olivia said, throwing a pine needle at him like a dart.

Zack held the bottle up and studied the remaining water.

"What? Are you checking for backwash?" Olivia said, offended.

"No," Zack said, "but you can never be too

careful." He tipped his head back, holding the bottle a few inches over his open mouth.

"My grandpa has a compass," Olivia said. "I should have brought it with me."

"WAIT!" Amp shouted. "DON'T DRINK THAT, ZACK!"

Zack froze. The water was just an inch from the opening of the bottle. His mouth hung open. "Why?" he grunted.

"We need that water to make a compass," Amp said.

"How can you make a compass out of a water bottle?" Olivia asked.

"Can I just have a teeny sip?" Zack said, licking his lips.

"After we use it to make a compass," Amp said. "I promise."

"I still don't get it," Olivia said. "How does a bottle of water tell you which way is north?"

Amp walked in circles on his paper stage. "Zack, do you remember I once told you the Earth is like a giant magnet?"

Olivia's hand shot into the air like she was in class. "Oh!"

"Yes, Olivia," Amp said, impressed at Olivia's enthusiasm.

"I remember this: The earth has lots of melted iron inside," Olivia said. "And iron is magnetic. All that iron makes the Earth one big magnet." She smiled at Zack.

"Show-off," Zack said. "But it's molten iron, not melted."

"Same difference," she said snootily.

"You are both right," Amp said, nodding. "The Earth is like a giant magnet hanging out there in space. And just like every magnet, it has two opposite poles."

"A north pole and the south pole," Olivia said.

Zack groaned. "I remember all this. One pole has a positive charge and one pole has a negative charge."

"Exactly," Amp said, snapping his fingers. "The north has the positive charge. Now all we need to do is suspend a magnetized needle in water and it will point to the way we need to go."

"Sounds great," Olivia said, "but we don't have a needle."

"Well, then it's time to get creative," Amp

said, rubbing his hands together.

"Attention Erdian Council . . ."

Amp was speaking into his tiny wrist recorder. "Not again!" Zack growled. "I'm getting eaten alive by mosquitos and will soon get eaten by bears or werewolves! Can you please do that later?"

Amp cleared his throat and turned his back to Zack.

"Humans have a general understanding of magnets and the Earth's own magnetosphere, but are completely untrained in using the resources around them to help themselves."

"You know we can hear you, right?" Olivia said. Amp looked back at Olivia and continued.

"I must teach the children how to think for themselves, be creative, and apply their general scientific

**knowledge in a practical way. Will
report on the results later."**

Amp turned back to the children, raised his little chin, and smiled.

"You won't report anything if we all get eaten first," Olivia said.

14

Junk Pile

Following Amp's instructions, Zack and Olivia emptied the contents of their pockets.

They had Olivia's water bottle, a dime, two pennies, a small plastic container of mints, a message from a fortune cookie, a paper clip, a rubber lizard, a cheap pair of headphones, a plastic hair clip, pocket fuzz, the paper wrapper from a sugarless piece of gum, and four slightly smashed and dusty gummy bears.

Amp picked up one of the gummy bears and began nibbling on its head as he looked over the humble stockpile. "Not much to work with here," he said, talking with his mouth open.

"Don't smack," Olivia said, frowning.

"This pile of junk is no help," Zack sighed.

"We're sunk," Olivia said, her voice sounding

higher and tighter than it had all day. "It'll be dark soon. Really dark."

The light was indeed starting to fade. Zack glanced up. The clouds he could see between the treetops were now turning a dark violet.

"We can do this," Amp said, biting a foot off his gummy bear.

"How so?" Olivia asked.

Amp dropped the gummy bear, brushed off his hands, and handed the paper clip to Zack. "Quick, twist that around till the small, straight end breaks off."

"What's it for? To pick your teeth?" Zack asked.

"That will be our compass needle," Amp said. "It's the most important part of the compass we're about to make. That paper clip is made of steel wire, so we can magnetize it."

"I thought iron was the best metal for a magnet," Zack said, recalling a bit of information about his science experiment from so many weeks ago.

"Yes, pure iron is best. But that steel is an alloy of mostly iron and a little bit of carbon. Perfect for an improvised magnet."

"Improvised?" Zack said.

"That's just a fancy way of saying Amp's making this up as he goes," Olivia said.

Zack finished twisting off the end of the paper clip and held it up. "Which way is north, paper clip?"

"Don't be ridiculous," Amp said, shaking his head. "I can see I have more to teach you about science *and* about thinking on your feet."

"But I'm sitting on my butt," Zack said, confused. "Do you mean you need to teach me about thinking on my butt?"

"Seriously?" Olivia said to Zack. "What's next, Amp?"

Amp took the lid off the round, plastic container of mints, which looked like a miniature green hockey puck. He then flipped it over with his foot, sending a dozen tiny white mints scattering into the dirt.

"Hey!" Zack protested. "Those are mine!" He picked a few out of the dirt, blew them off, and popped them in his mouth. "I'm starving!"

"So gross," Olivia said, shaking her head.

Zack grabbed two of the dusty gummy bears and threw those into his mouth, too. "I could eat a real bear right now. I'm so hungry."

Amp flipped the green mint container back over with a grunt. "Okay, Olivia, now break open one of those headphones. There should be a small magnet inside."

Without hesitation, Olivia broke open one of the earpieces by smashing it on a nearby rock, easily splitting the plastic in half with a loud *crack*!

"Hey, my headphones!" Zack howled. "Could we stop destroying my stuff, please? I'm the one who contributed the lizard!"

"That rubber toy is of no use," Amp said, "but most speakers—even headphone speakers—have a small magnet inside. He took the tiny black piece of metal that Olivia plucked from the speaker and studied it. "Zack, rub this side on the paper clip, but only in one direction. And lift it away from the paper clip after each stroke. We need all the magnetic moments in that steel pointing in one direction. Count the magnet swipes out, all the way to one hundred."

"So the north end of our magnet will point to the north pole, right?" Zack said, feeling proud of himself for getting it.

"No, not exactly," Amp said simply. "While the north pole of the Earth is indeed the geographic north, it is actually reversed when it comes to this planet's magnetic poles. They're opposite. So the Earth's northern pole is actually the southern pole magnetically. Get it?"

"My brain just exploded inside my skull," Zack said quietly.

Olivia nodded. "So the north pole of our paper clip magnet will point to the southern pole magnetically, which is north geographically?"

"Exactly!" Amp cried, clearly impressed by Olivia's grasp of magnetism. "Remember, opposites attract when it comes to magnets."

"Forty-five, forty-six, forty-seven, forty-eight," Zack growled, rubbing the magnet over the paper clip again and again.

"Okay, Olivia, please pour some of your water in here," Amp said, pointing to the now-empty plastic mint container.

Olivia carefully filled it with water.

"Now we need something to float our paper clip on," Amp said, picking up the paper gum wrapper and studying it.

"How about a flower petal?" Olivia said, picking up one of the flower petals she had dropped earlier.

"Perfect," Amp said. "Lay it flat on the water. Understand, this planet's magnetism is actually quite weak, so we need to remove as much resistance as we can, so the paper clip can swing around easily. There will be very little friction in this setup."

Olivia placed the petal on the water surface. It floated perfectly. "So pretty," she said.

"One hundred!" Zack said, holding up the paper clip. "Done!"

"Okay, now look, the southern end of our magnet has a little bend in it," Amp noted, pointing to the piece of metal. "The northern end is the perfectly straight end. So, Zack, gently place our pointer on this floating petal."

Zack dropped the piece of paper clip onto the petal and the three of them stared at their tiny contraption. Then, as if by magic, their tiny paper-clip-and-flower-petal boat rotated slowly and pointed directly at Zack.

"Whoa," Zack whispered. "That's amazing."

"It worked," Olivia said, her eyes fixed on their makeshift compass. "But still, which way is north?"

"What do you mean, which way is north, Lost 'Livia? It's clearly pointing that way!" Zack gestured in one of two directions the compass was pointing.

"But what if it's *that* way?" Olivia demanded, pointing in the opposite direction.

"Olivia's right, Zack," Amp said. "Our paper clip didn't exactly come pre-magnetized with its north pole painted red for us. We do know that one end is pointing north, and the other is pointing south—we just don't know which is which. We need another reference to give us a clue."

"I'm out of clues," Zack said, rubbing his eyes as the sun emerged from the low hanging clouds to illuminate the horizon before disappearing below it. Olivia looked in the direction Zack was rubbing his eyes.

"The sun!" she exclaimed. "It sets in the west!"

"But it's gone already," said Zack. "We're still stuck with a compass with the accuracy of a coin toss. We're sunk."

"It's OK, all we need is a general direction of where west is," said Amp. "Which side of the compass was the sun setting on?" he asked.

"Left side," said Zack.

"Ooh!" Olivia shouted. "I remember now! Soggy waffles!"

"What?" Zack and Amp exclaimed together.

"This is no time to ruminate on odd dietary interests." Amp frowned.

"Speak for yourself, SweeTart breath." Zack chuckled.

"No, I'm remembering the directions from the compass rose. Never Eat Soggy Waffles—north, east, south, and west, in clockwise order. If we point our left arms west, we'll be facing north— and we'll know which end of the paper clip we should follow home!"

"Brilliant!" Amp squeaked.

"Huh?" said Zack.

"The end of the paper clip with the tiny bend in it, that's north!" Olivia shouted.

"Attention, Erdian Council . . ."

Amp was speaking into his wrist recorder again.

"Mission accomplished! I have shown the humans the importance of a basic understanding of science, creative thinking, and using the materials around them in new and unexpected ways to achieve their goals. This is Scout—"

Olivia grabbed Amp up before he could finish his report.

"C'mon, let's go!" she shouted as she ran past Zack in the direction their tiny compass had pointed. "Last one back is a rotten egg!"

The movement and excited voices woke Smokey from his dog dream. He sprang up and shot after Olivia, barking as he went.

"WHOA! WHOA! Hey, you took the water bottle!" Zack called out after Olivia, but she didn't stop. Zack licked his dry lips, spun around, plucked the petal and piece of paper clip out of the mint container, and quickly drank the compass water. "Aaaah," he said, savoring every drop of the mint-flavored water.

He jumped to his feet, then stuffed the parts of the compass, their paper map, and the tiny magnet in his back pocket. He ran after Olivia and Amp.

"WAIT FOR ME!" he screamed as the last remains of the light quickly faded.

15

Lost and Found

They hadn't run more than ten minutes before they saw the bright glow of lights ahead.

Zack was just feet behind Olivia, and they were both breathing hard from navigating at full speed through a nearly ink-black forest.

Zack heard voices ahead. "We did it," he gasped as a tree branch snapped back and slapped him rudely in the face.

He ran into Olivia. She had stopped suddenly when she pushed her way through the last scrubby bush.

Zack peered over her shoulder and saw that campsite number thirteen was now a hive of activity.

There were easily thirty people standing around. Six green ranger trucks and five county

sheriff jeeps were parked at odd angles around the campsite. All the bright headlights and several floodlights on tripods forced the kids to shield their faces while their eyes adjusted to the brightness.

Zack could see several rangers leaning over a large map draped over the hood of one of the jeeps. One by one they looked up at the kids.

The buzz of voices steadily grew silent as the stunned crowd all took notice of the two mud-covered, panting kids who had entered the circle of light. Everyone froze. The only noise was the squawk of the police radios inside each of the vehicles.

Zack looked down.

Olivia was secretly holding Amp behind her back in a fist. She was nudging Zack so he'd take Amp. She was squeezing him too tight. It looked like his head was about to burst. Staying hidden behind Olivia, Zack took Amp from her hand and in one smooth movement stuffed his alien friend into his pocket.

Zack released a big sigh of relief; there was no way Amp's invisibility could work on this many people at once.

Smokey barked a greeting and that seemed to snap the crowd out of their stunned silence.

Zack's mom, dad, and brother burst out of the crowd and ran to them. Zack could see Mom had been crying and she had a large orange blanket wrapped around her. They all collapsed into a giant family hug with a laughing Olivia smashed in the middle. Mom was weeping in relief and Dad wiped tears from his face with the back of his hand.

"We thought you guys were goners," Taylor said.

"Oh, hush, honey," Mom sniffed. "Thank goodness you're both safe!"

"And Smokey, too," Taylor said, falling to his knees and hugging the dog. "We thought you'd run off with the bears, old boy!"

"Oh, my brave little boy," Mom said, hugging Zack so tight he thought his bones might break. Then she turned and put Olivia in a serious bear hug.

"This small army was about to head out into the forest to find you guys," Dad said, ruffling the hair on top of Zack's head. "They were just waiting for the bloodhounds to arrive."

Ranger Davis approached with a big smile on his face. "Well, this makes our job a whole lot easier! You're both all right? Nobody hurt?"

"I'm hungry," Olivia said.

"And I've got a wicked blister," Zack said, which brought a round of relieved laughter from the gathered crowd.

Everyone wanted to hear their story, so they walked over to the hood of the nearest ranger truck and Zack pulled out the pieces of their

compass and demonstrated it for everyone. It still worked.

"Wow," Ranger Davis said, clearly impressed with the two kids before him. "Two tough survivalists," he said, shaking his head in disbelief. "Gives me hope for the future."

Taylor stepped through the crowd and studied their small compass and looked a little jealous for all the attention his big brother was receiving. But he didn't say anything.

Soon the crowd began to leave the campsite after another round of well wishes.

Zack could see that a sturdy-looking temporary bridge had been placed over the creek where the wooden bridge had been washed away. It felt as if he'd been gone for a week.

Zack and Olivia each ate two hot dogs in two minutes, the hot food feeling great as it dropped down into their empty stomachs. They chugged on fresh water bottles. Zack let out a thunderous burp and almost felt like his old self again.

As the large temporary lights that had been set up around the campsite began to get switched off, they all piled into the car, which had been packed and prepped for a speedy escape.

They had only been there for one night, but nobody seemed to want to risk spending another one there. Clearly, everyone was ready to cut their losses.

The whole day had all been so exciting and intense, Zack almost failed to notice the foul smell in the car. At first he thought Amp—still hiding in his pocket—was trying to pull one of his mind-smell tricks, but Taylor set him straight before he could panic.

"That terrible smell is bear pee," Taylor explained. "They peed all over our car."

Zack smiled. "I guess it could have been worse, right?"

16

Science Geek

Three hours later, the car hummed through the night.

Zack sat quietly in the hushed car's rear seat for the rest of the ride.

Taylor was asleep and giggling occasionally, his grinning face pressed into Olivia's shoulder. Smokey jerked at Zack's feet, dreaming of who knows what. Dad snored softly every six seconds or so. Mom was hunched behind the steering wheel, concentrating on the road, like a determined mama bear rescuing her baby bears.

Even Olivia, who was sitting between Zack and Taylor in the backseat, had fallen asleep. Zack couldn't remember ever seeing her sleep before. She looked pretty normal, peaceful even. She was definitely not a McGee.

Zack watched Amp do push-ups on his knee in the shifting light from passing headlights. He was trying to get back in shape. Too many Swee-Tarts, Ritz Crackers, and gummy bears can make even an alien fat.

Zack thought about his friend and how his deep knowledge of science stuff had saved them. Zack loved how they had made that compass. It showed him that knowledge about the world around you could really be important, useful, and—dare he think it?—fun!

He had never considered science "fun" in his life.

Before this trip, science had always been boring stuff to be avoided, the blah-blah-blah you had to memorize for a quiz, not something that had to do with real life.

But now he knew differently. And he wanted to learn more. He shook his head at himself. "Science geek," he whispered.

Amp had flipped over and was now doing his weird Erdian version of sit-ups. It looked like an invisible hand was karate chopping his belly over and over.

Zack knew he might only have a few weeks left with his Erdian pal. He'd be heading home soon—either after the invasion or to stop it. But for now Zack wanted to learn whatever he could from Amp. And he was sure that Amp would jump at

the chance to show off.

He didn't know how, but the chance that he would become a scientist, or inventor, or engineer, or some kind of doctor when he grew up had mysteriously become a possibility—that is, if he didn't become a pro ballplayer.

He knew it was possible.

Zack looked out at the darkness and smiled. If Amp had taught him one thing, it was that anything was possible.

THE END

Try It Yourself: The Water Compass

You may already be familiar with a compass— the almost magic-seeming navigation device whose red-tipped needle always points north. They've been around for centuries, helping adventurers navigate since around the year 1000 AD. Compasses can be mesmerizing, whether you're holding one and spinning in circles as you watch the needle stay steady, or directing the needle back and forth with the invisible magnetic field from a nearby refrigerator magnet.

And one of the best parts about a compass is that it's so simple to build! In fact, you can build an improvised and fully functional compass out of parts you can find at home.

For this experiment, you will need:

- A paper clip
- A refrigerator magnet
- Something that's buoyant in water, like a piece of cork or Styrofoam (preferably with a flat side to it)
- A plastic bottle cap
- Water
- MOST IMPORTANT: An adult to help

1. To begin, unbend the first two curves of the paper clip. At the second curve, bend it back and forth lots of times until the metal "gets tired" (fatigues) and comes apart. Do your best to straighten the unbent piece. This will be the compass needle.

2. Now it's time to magnetize the needle just like Zack did. Hold the tip of the needle in one hand and the refrigerator magnet in the other hand. Holding the refrigerator magnet in the same orientation, drag it lengthwise down the needle, starting by your fingers and swiping right off the end. Bring the magnet back around for another pass without making contact with the needle until it's by your fingers again. Now repeat 99 times!

3. Your needle is now magnetized. Even though it's not a very strong magnet, it's still having some force exerted on it by the Earth's magnetic field. It wants to turn and align with the field, pointing north! The next step is to allow it to turn more easily by letting it float in the bottle cap. Break pieces off of your floaty piece (the cork or Styrofoam) until it's a little bit round and fits easily in the bottle cap. If it has a flatter side, put that side down toward the water. Poke the needle through the Styrofoam or cork so the needle is held steadily parallel to the bottom flat side. You might want an adult to help with this part.

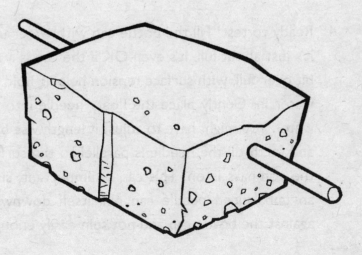

4. Ready to test! Fill the bottle cap with water until it's just about full. It's even OK if the cap is a tiny bit over-full, with surface tension helping hold the water in. Gently place the floaty needle into the water. You might have to adjust it lengthwise back and forth till the needle is parallel to the surface the compass is on. This can be important, since an unbalanced needle can pull itself downward against the bottle cap and not spin easily enough.

Test 1!

First, check to ensure your needle is magnetized. Bring the refrigerator magnet close by and swing it back and forth slowly around your compass. Does the needle spin? Great! Your compass is already showing you it can align to the magnetic field coming out of your refrigerator magnet! How far away can you hold the magnet and still make your compass spin?

Test 2!

Now take the refrigerator magnet far away from your compass. You should see the needle spin slowly to align itself north/south. Once it's aligned, try rotating the bottle cap underneath the needle. The needle should stay aligned to the Earth's magnetic field! Remember how far away your refrigerator magnet could affect the compass direction? It was probably on the order of about a foot, max. Now think: how far away from the north pole do you live? Probably pretty far. Think about how strong of a magnet the Earth's molten iron core is, to be able to point your compass needle from that far away! Pretty strong indeed.

Which way's north?

You've had success! Your needle is clearly aligning to Earth's magnetic field! But which way is actually north? Without some other point of reference to compare to, you don't exactly know which end of your needle you should paint red so you can tell north from south when you're out in the field. You can use another compass, or a map and a geographical feature, to give yourself a reference point. By comparing an approximate direction you know is north to where the needle is pointing, you should easily be able to tell which end of the needle is pointing toward magnetic north. Zack, Olivia, and Amp used the sunset to reference an approximate direction for west, which will always be to the left of the compass needle.

Troubleshooting:

A compass is a sensitive instrument, meaning not only can it detect faint signals like a faraway magnetic field, it can also be interfered with easily by other things you're not trying to measure. Here are some things to think about if your compass isn't working exactly as expected:

- Make sure your needle is magnetized. You should see the needle moving when you wave your refrigerator magnet nearby. If it's not wiggling around in response to the magnet, swipe the magnet down the length of the needle in one direction a lot more times.

- If the needle can't spin easily, it won't be able to point north/south, because the forces exerted on it by the Earth's magnetic field are very small. Make sure the Styrofoam or cork float isn't crashing into the edges of the plastic bottle cap. Try adjusting the water level as well, to make sure it's centered.

- Check to make sure the needle is parallel to a horizontal surface, like a table.

- Just like the refrigerator magnet's magnetic field is strong enough to override the Earth's magnetic field effects on the compass needle, other fields from nearby objects might also interfere. Make sure there are no other magnets or large pieces of steel nearby. A pair of headphones, a cell phone, or even a cookie sheet can mess up your compass's sensitivity if they're too close. Isolate your compass to get a good reading.

- Make sure the needle is nice and straight.

What's actually going on here?

Magnets are crazy! Isn't it cool how you can hold a magnet in each hand and feel the forces they exert on each other right through your skin and bones, without even being able to see anything? Believe it or not, magnetic fields can be produced in a few different ways, and even completely natural rocks can have permanent magnetic fields just like the magnets on your refrigerator.

There are a few different types of magnetism, but the kind we encounter most often is called "ferromagnetism." The "ferro" part stands for *iron*, which is present in both the Earth's core and in the steel that makes up much of our engineered world, including paper clips.

In the atoms of the ferromagnetic material, like the paper clip, the tiny particles called electrons each act a little bit like tiny magnets themselves. When they get stuck together and form a lump of material, groups of them tend to align themselves in the same direction. We call those "magnetic domains." It would be like if you were in a classroom at school, and everybody split into groups of friends who were each looking at different parts of the room. When the teacher says "pay attention up front please!" and all of the groups face forward, it's like the classroom got magnetized! It's just that to magnetize the compass needle, you have to have the "teacher" (the refrigerator magnet) ask the "class" (the electrons and magnetic domains) to all face the front about 100 times in a row before they all pay attention.

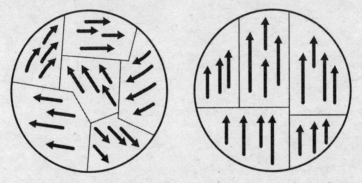

To learn more, look up some articles about ferromagnetism. You can use your compass to help you navigate to the library! And while you're there, check out *Alien in My Pocket: The Science UnFair* to read about Zack's adventures building magnets that run off of electricity. Electromagnets!

Telescope Troubles

01

Brain Dump

Okay, I'm just going admit something right from the start: I've had an alien no bigger than a soda can secretly hiding in my bedroom for the last few months.

You might think that it'd be an amazing thrill— but you'd be mistaken.

I've seen and done things that nobody in human history ever has. I started a city-wide panic and successfully launched a spaceship into orbit out of my own backyard, and I created an electromagnet strong enough to nearly destroy a city building—all to prevent an alien invasion of planet Earth.

It's been a pretty hectic and stressful few months.

And to be perfectly honest, it's been a lot for a fourth-grader to handle.

I've had trouble sleeping. My grades have suffered. I dislocated my shoulder. It still clicks when I raise my hand. I had to erase my little brother's short-term memory, and now he seems weirder than ever. I almost got eaten alive by a pack of bears. Oh, and I've had to smuggle about four hundred tons of Ritz Crackers and SweeTarts into my room. Amp, my houseguest from the planet Erde, has some odd ideas about food and nutrition.

My parents are convinced I have mental issues, because they often catch me talking, laughing, and arguing in my room—and they think I'm alone! Mom's even taken me to Dr. Bell's office twice now for "a chat," but he just told her that I was sleepy and slightly confused, but an otherwise perfectly ordinary kid.

If he only knew . . .

There have also been a few more unexpected side effects caused by playing host to an alien. For example, actually knowing a real-life alien totally ruins every movie you see about aliens! And it changes the way you think about Earth: we are *so* not the center of the universe. Most important, it answers the age-old question about whether life exists on other planets—it does, and I have the roommate to prove it.

All this makes evenings like tonight extra special.

See, tonight is my night off. Amp is hanging out with Olivia, my next-door neighbor, classmate, best friend, and the only other person on the planet who knows about the alien hiding out in the McGees' house.

Twice a week Olivia babysits Amp. Or, more accurately, she prevents him from starting a worldwide panic while I get some quality alone time.

What do I do while he's away? These blissful few hours of peace and quiet are often spent cleaning my room—Amp makes a serious mess. Ritz Cracker crumbs and dust are everywhere.

He eats them like a termite eats wood. Sometimes I nap. Sometimes I just stare at the wall and let my brain relax. Like I said, hiding an alien from your parents and little brother can be pretty mentally exhausting.

As the sun dips below the garage roof outside my second-story bedroom window, I fall into a herky-jerky sleep, dreaming about eating a salami-and-worm sandwich in front of my class—it's my brain's favorite weird dream and one I've actually grown to enjoy.

Of course, that nap was the beginning of the end of Amp's time here on Earth.

This is the story of how I let my guard down and how my nosy little brother stepped in and the world as we know it nearly ended.

02

Meltdown

Apparently, I didn't feel the first few Milk Duds bounce off my face.

It wasn't my fault. I was sound asleep.

Then one of the chocolate candies hit me square on the front tooth with a loud *click*. I sat up like startled cat.

I blinked in the dim light, trying to make sense of what had hit me.

I picked up the Milk Dud in question and stared at it like it was a bullet from another universe. I put a finger to my tooth and gave it a wiggle to see if the flying candy had knocked it loose.

My sheets, blankets, and pillow were covered with about forty Milk Duds. I popped one in my mouth and started chewing slowly.

Another candy zipped through the dim light

5

out of nowhere. I was slow to duck—and blink. It beaned me square in the open eye.

"Ouch!" I shouted, pressing a palm to my stinging, watering eye.

I scrambled to the window. The flying candies were coming through the big hole in my window screen. I could see Olivia down in my backyard, eating from and holding the biggest box of Milk Duds I had ever seen.

"Why are you throwing Milk Duds at my face?" I hissed. "You almost blinded me!"

"I called, but your mom told me your doctor says you need to sleep more. She said you might have a sleeping disorder."

"I do," I said. "His name is Amp!"

The night sky was sparkling with stars. The little bulb by our back door was on, so I could see Olivia well enough to know something was on her mind.

"What do you want?" I asked. "You're supposed to be babysitting till eleven thirty. Is it eleven thirty already?"

She pushed a wad of half-chewed Milk Duds to the side of her mouth with her tongue. She now looked like a distracted squirrel. "Something happened," she said from the other side of her mouth.

I stared down at her. "Something? Can you be more specific?"

"Something bad."

"How bad?" I said, shaking my head.

She paused, swallowed the gob of chocolate with some effort, and then looked around as if she were trying to figure out how to tell me the news. She sighed. "Amp kinda had a meltdown."

"What kind of meltdown? I didn't think aliens could even have meltdowns."

"I didn't think so either."

"Then what do you mean he had a meltdown?"

"It's like his spirit was broken."

I grabbed a fistful of my hair in frustration. "What does that mean?" I growled. "Olivia, what's wrong with you? First you almost knock my tooth out, then you nearly blind me, then you get all mysterious."

"Sorry," she said, blinking. Now she really did seem upset. She held up the box of candy. "I'm an emotional eater."

137

"Okay," I said. "Take it easy. Just relax. He drives me crazy, too. Where is Amp now?"

"I don't know."

"Is he nearby?"

"I don't know."

"Did he come back to my house?"

"I don't know."

"Which direction did he go?"

"I don't know."

"Was he going to get something?"

"I. Don't. Know."

"You're some babysitter! I hope you're not expecting a tip!"

Olivia looked down at her shoes. I thought she might start to cry.

"Okay," I said. "We'll figure this out. He gets touchy sometimes. When did this all happen?"

"About two hours ago."

"*What?* He's got a two-hour lead? He can't be out on his own! He can't be seen. He'll get eaten by a cat or a badger."

"I know that!" she shouted.

"Shhh! My parents . . . Why didn't you come get me earlier?"

"I told you, I tried! Your mom has you in sleepy time lockdown. I was trying to find him on my own so you could get your beauty rest."

I thought for a moment. "Okay, go get your grandpa's ladder. My mom is not going to let me out, not at this hour. We'll find him together."

Olivia nodded and walked off, looking relieved to have the beginnings of a plan, any plan, taking shape.

"And save some Milk Duds for me," I said, trying to make the situation less tense. I'm not sure if it worked. Olivia didn't look back. She disappeared into the hole in the fence between our two backyards.

I popped my screen out and dropped it into the bushes below. I looked around my room. An uneasy feeling overtook me. I quietly closed my door all the way. I could hear my parents talking excitedly down in the kitchen.

I turned back to my empty room. "Somebody remind me to strangle that alien when I get my hands on him."